The Princess

with

The Stinky Feet

This is a story about Princess Anne who was born with stinky feet. I know, right? I laughed too but for a Princess this was not so funny.

"Wait a second here," says Cicero, "I'll tell you how the story goes! As I was saying, it started one day when Princess Anne arrived. There seemed to be a lot of commotion going on over this little baby, Geez! Princesses! Princesses! …. everyone wants to be a Princess. Huh! Have I got news for you, it's not all it's cracked up to be!

Oh sure, on the outside it looks so regal and glamorous and so fantastic, right? .... Wrong! You see, people are people and no matter who you are or where you come from, you're going to have some problems. Everyone has problems and trust me this little girl has a doozy!" "Wait! Cicero, what about, well you know, you left out the part where it all really started." "Oh! Xavier why do you always have to butt in on everything?" "Excuse me but.... If you're going to tell the story you must tell it right!" "Ok ok fine, as I was saying...."

Andrea and Seraphina two teenage sisters were playing in a beautiful meadow laughing and joking running through all the wildflowers until they both fell to the ground and collapsed in a fit of giggles. "Andrea do you find Prince Malcolm handsome?" "Why?" "Well, I saw the way he looked at you and well I was wondering if you thought or felt that way about him?" Andrea starts to blush, "Do you think he does?" "Oh my God, you do!" ... "I didn't say." "You didn't have to." Andrea sees the look on her sister's face , "Oh no, do you like him as well Seraphina?" "No heavens no." They both just stare at one another not knowing what to say...Well it doesn't end there trust me.

Princess Anne's Arrival - Present day. The two nurses are in the nursery leaning over the baby's crib, but we only see the back of them and puffs of powder flying everywhere. There's an awful lot going on. Nurse Louise declares, "Have you ever seen such a beautiful baby?" "Oh, it's such a shame about her dreadful condition...." Nurse Weezy, "Shhhh! You're going to upset the Mrs." The nurses are feverishly applying lotion and powder and then wrapping her little feet swathed in fine cotton and as they finish, they remove the clothes pins from their noses. Nurse Weezy, "Ahhh, now that's better. Well now, shall we join the others? I believe she's ready." She lifts the little Princess out of her crib, places her in her bassinette and off they go to the dining room where Princess Anne's parents, King Malcolm and Queen Andrea are already seated at the table. As the maid serves breakfast, Queen Andrea asks, "How is our little Princess this morning?" Nurse Lucy replies "Oh, she's quite perfect your Majesty and she slept so sweetly just like a little Princess." King Malcom smiles, "Splendid, after breakfast we will address the people and put all the nasty rumors and fears to rest by showing them that our darling little Princess is just fine." Nurse Weezy answers, "Yes, as you will your Majesty," and as she continues tending to the Princess, the little precious baby smiles and coos contentedly.

We are now in the town square which is crowded with people and they are all anxious to catch their first glimpse of the new Princess. The crowd is stirring, and everyone is chattering amongst themselves when one man yells out, "I hear she is not right, they say something is the wrong with her," and yet another man announces, "Maybe she has four arms hahahaha!" A couple of women in the crowd are heard tattling to each other about the Princess being so ugly no one is allowed to see her or even look at her. Laughter is rippling through the crowd with all sorts of gossip flying through the air. A woman with a scarf covering her head and face suddenly leaves and it is quite clear she is upset as we watch her exiting the square with tears in her eyes. When the bugles sound, the crowd settles down and maintains an anticipated silence. The town crier appears and proclaims, "Ladies and Gentlemen of the Kingdom Bliss, I bring you King Malcolm, Queen Andrea and Princess Anne!" The crowd roars with excitement and cheers wildly as the Royal Party enter and take their seats on the balcony of the Palace. As the nurses enter with the Princess, King Malcolm and Queen Andrea address the crowd, "It is our greatest pleasure to introduce and present to you our beautiful daughter and your Princess, Her Royal Highness Princess Anne." The nurse lifts the adorable Princess out of her carriage and hands her over to Queen Andrea. The crowd gasps with relief when they clearly see the face of an angel smiling to her mother. One man exclaims, "Well, there's nothing wrong with her at all, she's quite beautiful!" A woman's voice rings out, "Oh my, she's quite lovely." The nurses exchange reassuring looks to each other. Yet another man in the crowd yells out, "She's a beauty but have you counted all her toes?" King Malcolm calmly replies with a smile, "Of course we have and yes, they are all there! You can see for yourself." The man cheekily retorts, "Well, we can't see anything with them all covered up." King Malcolm patiently answers, "My dear sir, she is covered up because she is a baby and we are in the middle of winter." An older woman nudges the man impatiently, "Yes, for goodness sake, what kind of an idiot would expose a child to the elements?" King Malcolm nodded, "Well said Ma'am, and with that we must now take our leave of you as it is time for the Princess to take her nap."

As they rise, they wave to the people and return to the warmth of the Palace.

Cicero meets the Princess...

It is nighttime in the Palace nursery and Cicero is peeking out of his little home waiting quietly to get a glimpse of the Princess when his friend Xavier tries to stop him. At that moment we see a figure standing over the crib but Nurse Weezy stirs, and the figure vanishes. Cicero whispers, "Hey did you see that?" "See what?" "It looks like someone was standing over the Princess." "No, I didn't see anything." "Huh! Really, could have sworn I saw someone!" However, Cicero being on a mission starts to head for the Princess, "I need to see what the heck is going on and what all this commotion is about with this little baby." "Are you out of your mind Cicero? Do you want to get yourself killed?" Cicero whispers, "Ahh, she's sleeping nothing is going to wake her up." Nurse Weezy is asleep in her rocking chair with her feet up and snoring her head off. Cicero sees that it is all clear and quickly crosses the floor from his little house and he climbs up on to the crib where the Princess is sleeping soundly. He peeks in at her with a cocky expression on his face but to his dismay, instead of discovering something shameful, he rests his eyes on the little Princess and sees a face of an angel sleeping peacefully. Cicero's heart melts and he immediately falls in love with the sight of the Princess. Suddenly, the snoring stops and Cicero freezes. Nurse Weezy sleepily walks over to check on the Princess. In a panic,

Cicero dives under the covers. Seeing everything is fine she returns to her chair and goes back to sleep. Cicero about falls over, breathes a sigh of relief and peeks out from the pillow just staring with complete adoration at the tiny Princess. "Well," says Cicero, "from the look of things you can tell where this is going."

The next day Queen Andrea and King Malcolm are in the study with Princess Anne and her nurse maids. A troubled Queen Andrea says, "Oh I hope this little problem is only temporary my dear sweet Anne. Oh Malcolm, please tell me it's so?" "Don't fret my dear, I'm sure it's only temporary and she.... she will grow out of it." The nurses both exchange a look of concern.

Time has passed and it's Princess Anne's 5th birthday and the Palace gardens are bustling with excitement. Balloons, pony rides, and all sorts of fun and exciting festivities for the children to enjoy. There are magicians and clowns performing tricks and making the children laugh. One of the magicians leans down and shows the Princess a trick and then whispers something into her ear and the Princess laughs. They stare at each other for an awkward moment when suddenly one of the children grabs the Princess's attention and they run off leaving the magician. Nurse Weezy and Nurse Louise are thrilled to see the Princess so happy...... Potter the Butler sounds the large bell which rings throughout the gardens to alert the children that he is about to announce something new. "May I have your attention, children?" The children stop chattering and look towards Potter. "Thank you, that's better. We are all now going to make our way to the Hall where we will gather for the cutting of the birthday cake. Now, who wants cake?" All the children jump up and down and dance with excitement yelling out, "Yes, yes, yes, cake, cake, cake, please!" When the children are all seated, they gasp when they see the beautifully decorated cake being rolled into the

Hall.   They all clap their hands and cheer wildly. Potter smiles solemnly as only a butler does and says, "Well then, shall we start?" The King and Queen watch happily while Princes Anne stands excitedly on her chair to see the cake. Her eyes are sparkling with happiness as Potter encourages the guests to sing Happy Birthday. Everyone enthusiastically sings Happy Birthday to the Princess and then Potter asks her to make her wish and blow out her candles. She makes her wish and blows out her candles to great applause. As the cake is being cut, disaster struck. Horror upon horror, the unthinkable happened! Princess Anne's shoe has somehow become torn, and her stockings are beginning to unravel around her feet but no one is aware of her plight. Cake is then eaten, and everyone is full. All the children return to the fun and games in the gardens. A little boy notices Princess Anne's shoe and stocking and mischievously decides to pull on it. With great horror he pinches his nose and screams out, "What is that awful smell, ughhhhh?" The Princess is immediately whisked away before anyone can say another word!

The Princess is laying on her bed crying as her mother enters, "Oh, my dear sweet Anne are you alright?" Sobbing she says, "Noooooo! I'm not! My whole birthday is ruined, and I hate my stinky feet. Why do I have this Mummy?" "Oh darling, I don't know but I'm sure you're going to grow out of it." "You keep saying that! But I'm not. They just keep stinking." The Queen just holds her as she continues to cry and her nurse maids bow their heads in sadness. Cicero just stares out of his mouse hole with tears in his eyes as his heart is broken for the Princess. "Oh, what a shame! She is so sad I have got to find a way to help her." Xavier retorts, "You're not think .... thinking what I'm thinking?" Cicero, "Maybe!" A frustrated Xavier, "Do you remember the mess we got into the last time we tried something with that.... that, well you know what I mean, Cicero?" "Well Xavier, that was our fault, so we just need to make sure we follow accordingly." "What do you mean accordingly? It's a trick to try and destroy you me and anyone else involved. Are you listening to me Cicero?" "Yes, I'm listening to you but if we can't find a way to help her soon.... then...then...just.... Maybe I WILL!" Xavier just shakes his head and looks helplessly at Cicero.... It's now nighttime and Cicero is watching the Princess sleep while he rests on her pillow. The Princess stirs and slowly wakes up but Cicero just sits there quietly. It's quite obvious that the two have already met. She opens her eyes sleepily and murmurs, "Hello Cicero, you're not tired?" Cicero replied, "No, I couldn't sleep I have been so worried about you!" Princess Anne frowns, "Thanks. I hate my feet!" Cicero cries, "No...no you don't hate your feet, this is just a little hiccup and we're going to figure this out. Believe me I'm on it and when Cicero is on a mission that mission will be accomplished, no matter how long it takes!" Princess Anne whispers, "Oh Cicero, what would I do without you? You're my very best friend!" as she yawns and falls back to sleep with Cicero curling up next to her.

Twelve years have passed...

Princess Anne is now seventeen. She is curled up on the window seat in the

Palace library as she reads a book to her friends Cicero and Xavier, "And with that he drew his sword and said off with the evil Witch's head." Cicero and Xavier are completely captivated by the story they both lovingly stare at the princes as she continues reading. The Princess closes her book and smiles. Cicero, "Hahahaha! Good show, that was so good I thought for a moment he was a goner and then boom. WOW!" "I know me too!" shrieked Xavier. Princess Anne laughs, "I'm so happy that you liked the story and I have something in mind for both of you tomorrow that you're going to love." Cicero questions, "Tomorrow? Don't you have to go to your Ladies brunch?"

Princess Anne remembers, "Ohhh crumpets, that's right, I do! Oh well then, shall we do it the following day?" "That's a date m'lady!" grins Cicero.

Queen Andrea and Princess Anne arrive at the Garden Luncheon where they greet all the guests who are joining the party. As the Royal Party takes their seats, the guests are then also seated. People are talking animatedly and laughing as delicious food and drinks are being served. The Queen and the Princess are seated at a table with their friends Harriet and her daughter Kate along with Eleanor and her daughter Miranda. Harriet asks politely, "How is our dear sweet

King, Andrea?" "He is quite lovely, thank you for asking and how is Charles doing?" Harriet replies, "Just as stuffed as his shirt." They all laugh, and Harriet continues, "Speaking of stuffed shirts, why doesn't Anne go with Kate to the polo match this coming Saturday?" Queen Andrea nods and thinks that is a fabulous idea. "What do you think Anne? The Princess hesitates, "Umm, umm, yeah." Her mother shoots her a look, and the Princess understands she must be respectful and humbly replies, "Of course, I would love to go." Harriet chimes in, "Well then that's settled, you do know Prince Albert will be attending the Match?" Princess Anne is not impressed.

Queen Andrea suggests "Why don't you girls go and have a look at the desserts?" The girls agree, and they get up from the table and cross to the other side of the room. Miranda leans into Kate and whispers something about Princess Anne. They both start to laugh when the Princess looks at them and they both compose themselves very quickly. Miranda walks to the other end of the dessert table while Kate and Anne stand together. Kate shows some concern, "I wouldn't pay any attention to her, she doesn't mean it." Princess Anne shrugs her shoulders, "Yes she does, she always has!" They both just stare at each other, and Kate realizes that the Princess is nice. "Yeah, your right,

I'm so sorry Anne." "It's ok, she's always been that way towards me." "Well maybe Miranda wishes she was a Princess too?" "Oh! Believe me if she spent one day in my well …. my shoes, she would be begging to be herself again." Kate looks quizzically at Anne, "Really, why do you say so?" "It's a long story and I won't bore you with the details." They both smile and the Princess excuses herself as Queen Andrea waves her daughter to return to the table. Kate waits for Miranda before joining the others. Miranda approaches Kate and demands, "Why were you talking to the Princess?" "Why shouldn't I talk to her Miranda?" "Well, umm …… she's just…… well, she's just strange."

"Miranda, that's not very nice, you sound mmmm......well you sound rather jealous." Protesting her innocence Miranda exclaims, "Jealous? Why would I be jealous of someone like that? Don't be ridiculous!" The two of them return to the table where they finish brunch and go home. A lovely lady wearing a beautiful hat smiles mischievously as she has been listening to the girls and watches them walk back to their table.

Cicero has been waiting for the Princess to come home and is now finally alone with her and asks how the brunch went while the Princess prepares for bed. Cicero joins her in her room anxious to know if she enjoyed the luncheon. "It was ok...well...hmmm...not really. Cicero do you remember Miranda, Harriet's daughter?" Cicero pouts, "You mean the little girl who would pull everyone's hair including yours?" They both laugh. Princess Anne agrees, "Yes that's her. I don't think she likes me ... In fact, I know she doesn't like me!" "Well Anne, you do know that you can't be friends with everyone as there is always going to be that certain someone who puts a damper on things. You just have to shrug it off and pay no attention to it, It's her problem not yours." "I know Cicero, but I do feel uncomfortable to be around her and I must see her this weekend at a polo match which, by the way, is why I don't want to attend. I would much rather stay here with you!" Cicero smiles at the Princess, "Well, maybe it will do you good to spend some time with people of your own age and besides, isn't the ball coming up soon? Why, you might even meet a nice handsome young lad." "Oh, I doubt that, one whiff of my feet and its curtains for me! I have given up on that dream since I have been cursed with this dreadful condition. Anyway, I cannot do a thing about it, so I now just accept my fate." "Anne, what on earth are you talking about? You can't just give up on life because of some stinky feet …… why, that's not right! You listen here, you are going to have a great life, of that I am sure, and if anyone doesn't like your feet then I don't like them either and that means they did you a big favor. The right person will love everything about you, including your feet." The Princess stares lovingly at Cicero admiring his loyalty, "Oh Cicero, what would I do without you?"

Anne's now in her dressing room with Nurse Weezy and Nurse Louise helping her to get ready for the Polo Match. Nurse Louise remarks to Nurse Weezy that Prince Albert is playing, and nurse Weezy adds, "He's quite the catch." Princess Anne sighs, "We know that's never going to happen for me as long as I have these feet. I am destined to live a life alone." Nurse Weezy and Nurse Louise look at each other with great sadness. Nurse Louise "Now my dear child, don't be silly there is someone for everyone." The Princess looks wistfully at her nurses, "Not with this condition!" An awkward moment of silence is shared, "Well, don't worry I still have all of you including Cicero and Xavier." She looks over at the two of them who are playing a game of chess and winks, "What more could a girl ask for." Nurse Weezy smiles and shakes her head.

Polo Match Day is here and the crowd, the horses and the riders are all filled with excitement for the big event. Prince Albert is already on his horse looking very dashing. Princess Anne is standing with Kate when Miranda approaches them exclaiming "Wow, what a surprise, the beautiful Princess has actually graced us with her presence." Kate raises her voice "Miranda!" "I was just saying that we never see her, and I am surprised she came." Kate replied, "I am delighted to see her again." Anne quickly tells them both that she's been very busy lately and Miranda sneers. "Yes, we know. Oh, there's Blythe, I must go and say hello to her. See you later." "Oh, I'm sorry Anne, she is so well...rather rude," "No, what I think you really want to say is that she's mean but its ok I'm not going to let it bother me Kate." She smiles and looks out at the field where the match is taking place and asks, "Shall we take our seats then? Kate nods, "Yes, that's a great idea." As they take their seats in the Royal Box, Prince Albert rides by on his horse and nods to the girls, "Oh my Anne, did you see him? He is so handsome!" Princess Anne notes Kate's enthusiasm and cautiously answers, "He's ok." A surprised and somewhat puzzled Kate challenges her, "You're joking right?" "No! No, I'm not he looks rather boring to me." The match begins, the excitement is bubbling, and the crowd enjoys a spectacular well fought game. Prince

Albert is joyous as his team won in a very tight match. Beaming, he strolls into the Polo Lounge where everyone is congregated having food and drinks and meeting and greeting their friends. His Royal Highness spots the girls and ambles over to them. He smiles happily and greets the Princess and Kate warmly, shaking their hands and asking, "Did you young ladies enjoy the match?" Princess Anne graciously replied, "Yes, it was quite exciting and by the way, congratulations on your win." Kate gushes, "Yes! Yes! Congratulations! You were so spectacular." It's obvious that Kate has a huge crush on Prince Albert. "Thank you ladies, we all just had a jolly good old time out there.

Are you two attending the dance tonight?" Anne and Kate both blurt out together, "Yes" …. "No." Laughing, Prince Albert asks, "Well, which one is it, yes or no?" Princess Anne can see that Kate is over the moon with Prince Albert and she carefully explains, "What we actually meant is that Kate is definitely going but unfortunately, I will not be able to attend as I have a prior engagement this evening." I am sorry to hear that you will not be attending Anne, but I will hopefully see you later Kate. It was nice talking to you," and he walks off to join his friends. "Oh my gosh, he is magnificent Anne." "He seems to like you too Kate." Do you really think … Oh but he wouldn't possibly…

well I'm not a Princess!" "We're all Princesses Kate, right here where it counts." as she places her hand on her heart. Kate is overwhelmed by Princess Anne's warm and giving heart and says softly, "Thank you Anne. Are you sure you won't come tonight? It would be so much fun, and I would love for you to come with me." "Oh, I don't know Kate, I get rather bored with these events. Oh well what the heck, maybe for you I will." "Really? Wow, this is going to be so much fun. I do believe we are going to have the best time ever. I can't wait. I will meet you at the Palace at 6.45 this evening. Bye for now!" "Ok, I don't know what I have gotten myself into, but I will see you then." They both head for home.

Cicero is watching Princess Anne putting her final touches to her outfit and her hair. He is so puffed up with pride and cannot help but admire how beautiful she is. "Wow! You look absolutely stunning …. mmm … mmm … mmm … mmm … mmm …" "Do you really think so Cicero?" "Does a mouse have fur?" The Princess chuckles with delight, "Oh Cicero, only you! Don't forget we have that reading date tomorrow." "Are you kidding me, I wouldn't miss it for the world." "Great, then I will see you later tonight." As she leans down to kiss Cicero on top of his head, he melts. Cicero whispers softly to himself, "Be safe my dear sweet Anne." Princess Anne is in the reception hall when she hears Kate ringing the bell. Kate enters looking beautiful and Anne remarks upon how much she loves her dress. Kate thanks her, "Oh my, you look gorgeous too! I really love your dress." Princess Anne smiles graciously, as they both leave. Princess Anne and Kate arrive at the ball and upon entering the ballroom, they are met with the glorious sounds of music and laughter everywhere. The Princess looks very happy to be with her friend Kate. The atmosphere is electrifying. The guests are dancing to wonderful music, eating delicious food, drinking and talking excitedly amongst one another. A couple of boys ask the girls to dance which they accept eagerly and join the rest of the guests on the dance floor having the time of their lives. Having danced for a long time, they decided they were ready for some serious refreshments. While they were waiting for their drinks to be served, Kate exclaims with utter joy, "Oh Anne, I'm so happy you came tonight." "Me too, I'm having great fun." As Prince Albert walks up and invites Princess Anne to dance poor Kate looks so dejected. "Actually Albert, I'm rather tired so perhaps you would like to dance with Kate?" A beaming Prince Albert replies, "Why, I would love to! Would you care to join me for this dance?" He offers a radiant Kate his arm and as they take to the dance floor, Kate's face glows and lights up a thousand times ... In the meantime, Miranda sneaks up on the Princess and taps her on the shoulder, "Why! Aren't we so lucky to be seeing so much of you these days!" Princess Anne miserably replies, "I guess so." Miranda relentlessly taunts the Princess, "If I can remember correctly, wasn't it you that had that condition on your feet? In fact, wasn't it at your birthday party and may I dare to ask, how is that dreadful condition Princess?" "It's fine Miranda! Don't you have something better to do?" "As matter of fact, I do... Tata for now!" Miranda walks off to another table and as she does, she notices that the Princess's feet are completely covered. The sly smile comes over Miranda face, "What a strange thing, most of the girls are wearing open-toed shoes for the ball. Hmmm!" Soon a laughing and happy Kate and Albert return from the dance floor. Kate breathlessly tells Prince Albert "That was simply wonderful" He nods with a smile and tells her he will catch up with her later. Princess Anne wants to go home and tells Kate that she is a little tired and will be leaving early. "Are you sure Anne? What's wrong. Is everything ok?" "Oh yes, I'm just a bit tired. You don't mind, do you?"

"No of course not. Anne thank you for all that you did for me tonight. I would never have danced with Prince Albert if it weren't for you." She gives Anne a big hug and the Princess turns to leave. Miranda stares at Anne as she leaves and it's obvious that she is up to no good as she walks over to Kate and spitefully sneers, "What's wrong with your new best friend?" An exasperated Kate answers sharply, "Miranda, what is your problem? She is a very nice person and why are you being so mean to her?" "Maybe I don't like fake people Kate." She's not fake." "Oh really, do you remember the stinky feet rumor about her? Well, I happen to think it's true and I am I'm going to find out and prove it to the world!" "Miranda!" Miranda retorts, "What?" Kate sternly warns her, "Don't you dare do anything bad." Miranda defiantly quips, "I'm not doing anything bad I'm just finding out the truth!" Kate walks away and Miranda stares with an evil smile on her face.

The Princess is now in her pajamas while sitting on her bed talking to Cicero about the Ball "I wish I hadn't gone. At first, I was having fun but then Miranda came up and asked me if I still had that same problem that I had at my birthday party." "Ah! She knew?" "I'm not all the way sure Cicero, but it sure seems like it. What am I talking about, of course she did. I knew by the way she said it. I felt so bad I just wanted to leave …. So, I did." "Oh Anne, I'm so sorry. She's obviously a very hateful mean girl and unfortunately you had to come up against her." Cicero shakes his head, "Nevertheless, don't give her two seconds thought because you're much bigger and better than that." "Thanks Cicero." "Besides, if she tries anything, I'll kick her bottom from here to France." They both burst out laughing.

Well now, little Miss Miranda is at home in her room after the Ball where she is pacing impatiently and mimicking the Princess, "Hi! Oh me, oh yes, I am the beautiful Princess,

and everyone please look at me."
"Bah! I'll look at you alright! Soon everyone will know you're a fraud and nothing but a stinking fraud. I am going to expose your dirty little secret and everyone will know that your nothing but damaged goods. You will be the laughing stock of the Kingdom. Then, I will become the special one and everyone will notice all my beauty!" Miranda slams her pillow down and glares into space as if she is in some evil trance.

Miranda Goes to The Woods...

As she is walking through the woods she comes upon the Witch's house. She knocks three times and the door opens on its own. The Witch asks,

"Who goes there?" "My name is Miranda." "Daughter of Eleanor?" "Yes, how do you know?" "I know everything that goes on in these here parts so state your business and why you're here." "Princess Anne has a little problem which I want to expose." The Witch appears from the dark very quickly and a little fear crosses Miranda's face. The Witch asks "Why?" "Because she is a liar to all the people." "Ha! you do know that it is I who cast the spell for her dreadful condition and it is I who decides what happens. However, let me hear what you have to say." Miranda reveals her plan to the Witch, "I want all the people to know she has this problem." The Witch cunningly says, "Oh do you? Why is that?" "Because people need to know the truth, she's not a perfect Princess." The Witch walks around her looking her up and down and Miranda becomes very uncomfortable, "Because the people need to know that you are?" "Exactly!" "Evil little jealous thing we are, love it! I will give you something but, you will have to come back in three days time, and you must tell no one." "I won't." "Very well, you're excused." Kate happens to be passing by on her horse when she spots Miranda leaving the Witch's house. Kate then takes her horse in the opposite direction.

A concerned Kate races to tell the Princess.

The Princess is reading to Cicero and Xavier from her window seat in the study. "…… And as he did, something magical happened and all was well in the kingdom." "Oh, that was so nice. I like the part where the knights stand up for Tristan." "Yes," says Xavier, "that was the best part." Nurse Lucy enters the room, "I hate to interrupt this party but lunch is being served." Cicero and Xavier jump into Princess Anne's pocket as she stands up and walks out to the garden. The three of them are having lunch laughing, eating and having a great time when Potter the butler appears, "Excuse me

M'lady, Miss Kate has arrived and would like to speak with you." The Princess glances down at her feet and sees that everything is ok. Potter has Cicero and Xavier jump into their handheld carriage as Potter takes them. "I will send her in." Kate walks out to the garden and is seated with the Princess. "Hi Kate, what brings you here today?" "Oh dear.... I saw Miranda leaving the Witch's house and I think it might have had something to do with you." A startled Princess, "Me? What would it have to do with me? Well, I always knew that girl was not right but what on earth would she have in common with the Witch?" Kate grimaces and gives her an 'are you joking look?' and they both laugh. As Kate glances across the table, she notices a few small dishes, tiny cups and half eaten food. "What is all this?" At first the Princess doesn't know what to say but thinks quickly and states, "It's for a painting I'm working on . . . yes! …. Yes! I'm studying my muse, yes, my muse." "Gosh It must be a very small one then." "Yes, it is a rather small painting indeed, but It helps to have life like vision." Kate nods agreeing, "Yes, that makes sense." "So how did the rest of the dance go? Were you able to talk to Prince Albert?" "Oh my gosh! I almost forgot that's the best part. We danced all night and you're not going to believe it he wants to take me to the opera." "I told you he liked you." "It's all because of you Anne and I am forever indebted to you." "Don't be silly I am glad I was able to play match maker." The girls both chuckle.

Princess Anne tells Cicero About the Woods...

Cicero is chatting away with the Princess, "So Anne, how's your friend Kate?" "She is fabulous, and I think it's all working out for her and Prince Albert." "Wow! well then, I had no idea. Are you a little upset about this?" "Oh, heavens no, I couldn't be happier for her. In fact, I helped it happen." "This wouldn't have anything to do with your little problem, would it?" Princess Anne laughs "No I promise, but she did say that Miranda was visiting the Witch in the Woods." "The.... the.... the Witch? What do mean the Witch?" "Well, I guess there's a Witch in the woods and Kate thinks she went there on my behalf." "On .... on your behalf? Oh... oh... oh...This is not good oh no, this is not good at all!" "Cicero, calm down. What do you mean this is not good? Should I be worried?" Cicero has a very worried look on his face. "No... no... no everything is fine." "You don't look fine. In fact, I have never heard or seen you act like this." "Oh no, no no I'm fine." Cicero fakes a yawn, "Wow, I'm feeling so tired, I guess I'm going to turn in early," and he scampers off to his mouse house. Princess Anne giving him a funny look, reluctantly acknowledged his hasty departure, "Ok, see you in the morning."

Cicero quickly returns to the mouse house...

He scurries down the corridor entering the room where a beautiful mouse named George is resting in bed. "Hey buddy get up …. we've got big problems!" "What do you mean we've got big problems? "It's the Witch, she's here." George jumps up, "She's come to finish me off!" As George is pacing back and forth wringing his paws and rubbing his face he states, "We have to do something now!" "I'm on it George." "Ok, what's your plan?" "I'll tell you later." George panics, "That's because you don't have one, ohhh my gosh." "Calm down buddy!" "Calm .... calm you just come racing in here and give me the worst news of my life and you ask me to be calm?" "Maybe not, these things have a funny way of turning out you know, we just have to find that funny way." George has a look of terror on his face, "I'm dead!"

The next day Princess Anne arrives at the stables where she prepares her horse for a ride. She rides into the woods where she comes upon the Witch's house. She stops and just stares at it when suddenly she hears a woman's voice calling from behind, "Hello, my beautiful angel what brings you to the woods today?"

"What?" as she turns, she sees an elderly woman collecting berries. "Why are you here in the woods young lady?" "I was just riding and ended up here." "Why are you here?" "Oh, I love these berries here in these parts as they make for a great pie, you must try them." "Is this your house?" "No my dear are you lost?" "Well, no but I thought... never mind." "What is it child you seem to be distraught, is everything ok?" We can see an actual concern in the woman's face. "No, I'm fine. I guess I will be on my way now, do you need any help before I leave?" "Oh no my dear, I have all the help I need." Princess Anne bids her a good day and rides off. As Princess Anne disappears the old women transforms back into the Witch and starts laughing in a soft evil way. "Hahahhaha! You have no idea how much help I have Hahahahahaha!"

Back in the Mouse house Cicero walks into George's room as he is getting dressed. "Where are you going so early George?" George sighs "I'm going to face her once and for all." "The Witch?" "Yes, the Witch." "Huhhh! George you can't! Have you lost your mind and forgotten how powerful she is? She will destroy you. You're just not thinking clearly." "Look Cicero, she has already destroyed me and if she really is after the Princess, then I need to find out

why." "I'm coming with you George."
"No! It's too dangerous and you have
already done so much for me. I
couldn't live with myself if I cause any
more pain. It's settled." Cicero looks
completely defeated.

George is scampering through the
woods when he suddenly stumbles
upon the Witch's house. He sees an
open window and decides to crawl
through it and although the Witch's
back is turned, without missing a beat
she cries out, "Hello George, and how
is the life of a mouse treating you?"
"Actually, quite well." She quickly
turns and immediately traps him in a
cage setting him up on a shelf.
"You're just in time." "In time for

what, Witch?" "Soon you will know....
soon." She laughs in an evil low voice.
Three knocks are heard at the Witch's
door as it creepily opens on its own
once again and surprise, surprise, in
walks Miranda. "Do come in child."
"What have you got for me?" The
Witch maliciously answers, "Well
now, we have to agree to a few
terms." "You didn't say anything
about terms but what the heck?
What are the terms?" "If you fail to
complete the task then you will end
up a lonely old spinster with 9 cats
and a maid for the rest of your life."
"That's it? No problem, I don't plan
on messing up although I do hate
cats. Ok, where do I sign?" As she
signs the document, the Witch's cat

hisses at her. Miranda sticks her tongue out at the cat as she signs the scroll, and the Witch whispers, "That's a good girl." George is watching with a very worried look on his face. "You will need to throw this liquid onto the Princess's feet. After that, nothing will stay on her feet, and they will permanently stink." George gasps and his eyes are wide with fear. Gleefully Miranda chirps, "Good, then I will do it." "Now, take the potion and be on your way and remember our deal. Make sure you tell no one." Miranda grabs the potion and leaves the Witch's house. Quivering, George asks the Witch, "Why? Why would you do such a horrible thing to someone so innocent?" "I cast this spell on her at birth when her father, King Malcolm, sent me into exile and destroyed my family and burned down my place along with my life's work." "So, you hurt a child for that?" The Witch has a confused look for a second but replaces it with an angry one. "You George, of all people, should know better than to cross me. At least she's still a human because I could have done to her what I did to you. You see, I do have a heart." "Your heart is warped. You're not right!" "SILENCE! Stupid rodent before I throw you in a pot and boil you!"

Xavier is trying to talk to Cicero but, he is too preoccupied packing up some things and filling a pouch. "Will you please stop and listen to me you cannot fight that Witch she is much too dangerous, you mustn't go." "I have no choice I must help him because I cannot live with myself knowing the danger this poor man well …. mouse is in. Knowing that we put him there! So... Xavier please watch the Princess for me, and I will be back soon." "Ok, ok, be careful my friend." and with that Cicero leaves.

It's Princess Anne's Dance Class and Nurse Weezy is waking the Princess saying, "Good morning my sweet Anne, it's time for you to prepare for your dance lesson." "Oh alright." "I will meet you in the dining room to serve your breakfast." "Thank you Weezy." Princess Anne dresses quickly and gets ready for her dance class. She then heads for the dining room and after finishing a light breakfast she fetches her bike and rides to her class. All the girls are lined up in formation doing dance drills and as they finish Miranda stares at the Princess with a deceitful look on her face. When the dance class is completed, Princess Anne grabs her stuff and leaves. Miranda, looking very suspicious follows the Princess with the evil intention of using the dreaded Witch's potion. Unfortunately for Miranda, a woman passes by at the very moment she wants to put her horrible plan into action. The opportunity to throw the potion over the Princess came and went and an unsuspecting Anne mounted her bicycle and rode off.

Cicero darting through the woods...

Nearing the Witch's house he silently scopes out the perimeter and peeking around he finds a mouse hole which he disappears into. He scurries through a maze of little tunnels where he is confronted with lots of scary rats watching his every move. Finally, Cicero with heart pounding, finds an opening into the house. As he emerges, he sees the Witch brewing something in her big black cauldron and fear grips poor Cicero. He looks around the room and sees a cage up on the shelf and something tells him to investigate. As he climbs nervously up to the cage and looks under the cloth, he sees George. "Cicero, what on earth are you doing here?" At that moment the Witch traps Cicero. "What a naughty…. naughty little mouse. You made a very bad decision but oh, do I have something rather special planned for you." She laughs wickedly as she throws him into the cage to join George. "Oh man, she's worse than I thought. Don't worry we're going to get out of this." George tells Cicero, "The Princess is in great danger! That Miranda girl was here, and the Witch gave her a potion to put on her feet so that nothing will stay on them."

"WHAT! We have got to get out of here. When the Witch is asleep, we will escape." "Cicero, I would like to believe you pal, but it doesn't look good for either of us." "Well George, you will just have to have a little faith in your old buddy here."

Back at the palace Xavier rushes into Princess Anne's room and she anxiously questions him, "Where is Cicero?" "Cicero, umm, well yes, right Cicero hmmm." "Xavier, this wouldn't have anything to do with the Witch, would it?" "How did you know?" "I didn't until now, but you had better tell me everything you know right now!" "Oh boy! I'm in big trouble for this .... ok, well .... well, you see, we have this friend and ummm. You have never met him and he's quite shy. Actually, you see he's really someone else."   "Xavier, I don't understand, you're not making any sense! What friend?" Xavier nervously stumbles over his words in explaining to Anne, "Well, ummm, we used to have friends and family in Prince George's Palace and he was our friend just like us when the evil Witch cast a spell on him and turned him into a mouse." The Princess is alarmed, "Stop right there Xavier! She did WHAT?" "Like I said the ...." "I got that part! So, you mean to tell me that a man mouse, mouse man has been living in here with us?" Xavier nods his head and sighs, "Yep."

Princess Anne has a horrified look on her face and at that moment Kate arrives at the Palace. Potter announces Kate as she enters Princess Anne's room. "Oh my gosh Kate, you were right, Miranda is up to no good with the Witch." "Anne, are you sure?" "YES!" The Princess is babbling, "Well the man mouse, Cicero's friend, then Xavier ...." "Anne what are you talking about? Cicero? Xavier? .... slow down!" Xavier comes out of hiding behind Anne's back and waves to Kate. She just stares at him for a moment, "Aha! That explains the dishes. This is Cicero?" "No this is Xavier, Cicero is with the Witch." "He's with the Witch but he's your friend? Who is the man mouse?" "I don't know. I mean I do but I don't. Just trust me I need your help Kate." She just stares at Anne and Xavier for a moment then nods, "Ok, I'm in. What do we do?" "First of all, we need to find out what Miranda is up to and since she likes you, maybe you can try and talk to her." "I'll try but she has not been the friendliest since you and I have been doing things together." "Well please use your sleuthing capabilities Kate." "Alright, I will be back in a few hours. Wish me luck. Bye!"

As Kate goes to Miranda's House Miranda's mother Eleanor hears a knock at the door opens it and sees Kate and welcomes her in, "What a lovely surprise! Please come in. Miranda darling, won't you come down, your dear friend Kate is here to see you?" Miranda says, "I'm a little busy right now Mother." In a stern voice her Mother says, "Miranda, do please come down." Miranda can tell by the tone of her mother's voice that she means business and decides to come down. There is an awkward moment between all of them when Eleanor says, "I'll have some tea and cookies brought to the sunroom. Now, go on you two." As they walk into the sunroom Kate asks politely, "How have you been Miranda? I have not seen much of you. What have you been up to?" "Kate, what makes you think I'm up to something?" "I ... well

I ... was just wondering if everything was alright?" "Why wouldn't it be?" "Look Miranda, I did not come over here to upset you so if you want me to leave, I will." Miranda realizes she could be useful, "No .... no, no what I mean, I guess maybe I felt a little left out with you and Prin ... I mean Anne. Perhaps I have been a little hasty so let me make it up to both of you. Maybe the three of us could have lunch together? Shall we say Friday 12:00 noon?" "Yes, perhaps we can, I will let you know."

Back at the Witch's House Cicero has been feverishly trying to find an escape route and just as he starts to open the door the evil Witch slams it shut and wraps a chain around it. She then locks them in a room with her cat guarding them. "Naughty little boys we are, aren't we? Well, that is going to cost you both a pretty one... Pity.... Pity pretty hahaha!" Slamming the door on Cicero and George, the evil Witch leaves the room with an eerie cackle!

Kate returns to the Palace and advises Anne of the lunch date on Friday. "I'm not sure about it. She seems awfully strange so maybe it's not a good idea. I don't have a great feeling about it." "That is exactly why we have to go Kate because if she does have something to do with all of this, well then, we need to find out." "Ok, but if it starts to look bad then we are to leave at once, agree?" "That's fair. Go ahead and tell her we accept her invitation." The girls look at each other with an unsaid understanding.

Xavier is watching over Princess Anne while she sleeps, and he senses all is not well. He is right, Anne is having a horrible nightmare about the evil Witch who has captured her, locked her up and is about to feed Cicero to the black cat. She suddenly bolts upright in her bed and catches her breath. A startled Xavier asks, "Are you ok?" "No Xavier, I was having a nightmare .... I hope." The Princess is so distraught and Xavier just stares helplessly with complete empathy.

As Kate and the Princess arrive at Miranda's house, Kate reiterates, "Remember, if anything goes wrong, we just simply leave, ok?" "It's a deal." Miranda answers the knock at the door and invites them in. Kate is surprised, "Hello Miranda I wasn't expecting you to answer the door." Miranda replies, "It seems as though everyone is a little busy, please do come in. It's so nice to see you both and lunch will be served in the garden." They all head to the table where tea and sandwiches are being served. Everything appears to be going well and they are all talking happily over lunch when Miranda gets up to pour tea from the other table where there is an extra pot of cream. As lunch progresses, Miranda pours the girls another cup of tea but as she pours Kate's, she then reaches for the other creamer which she pretends to pour in her cup. However, instead she fakes a stumble and pours the potion all over the Princess's feet which causes all her stockings to unravel. Looks of shock and horror cross their faces for a second when misery upon misery, a foul-smelling odor wafts in the air. Miranda is the first to speak "What have we here, hmmm! Let me guess …. the Princess with the stinkiest feet, hmmmm …. there must be some mistake for a real Princess certainly wouldn't smell like that.

Hahahahahahah!" As Miranda laughs uncontrollably, Anne tries in vain to get her stockings back on, but nothing works, and she is completely distraught. Kate cries out, "Miranda what have you done?" Miranda echoes, "Miranda what have you done!" Please, can't you see she's a fraud?" Kate stands up angrily, "Anne lets go. We must tell someone." Miranda scoffs, "Tell someone! What could you possibly say? I had you over for lunch and spilled some milk on her stockings by mistake!" "You know what you did Miranda, and it has something to do with that evil Witch. I saw you leaving her house in the woods." Miranda has a look of shock on her face, "WHAT? No .... it's not true!" Kate shoots a look of disgust at Miranda as she grabs the Princess's hand who is now crying and barefoot.

Princess Anne and Kate are in the Princess's bathroom now while Xavier sits on the side of the tub watching his poor Anne soak her stinky feet in the water. This was the only way for them not to stink of a disgusting odor! Kate moans, "This is all my fault! I should have never agreed to have lunch with that crazy girl." "Please don't blame yourself Kate, I am the one that asked you to arrange it. If anyone is responsible here, it's me. Ohh, how I wish Cicero were here, he would know exactly what to do...... Oh, my poor sweet Cicero, I hope he's alright." At that moment Nurse Weezy knocks on the bathroom door "Anne is everything alright in there?" They look at each other wide eyed and Anne trembling sheepishly answers, "Yes .... I'm fine .... no worries." "Do you have someone in there with you Anne?" With a worried expression on their faces, Anne and Kate look at each other and Anne responds, "Ah ... yes, I'm in here with Kate." This makes Nurse Weezy open the door. "Oh my .... what have we here? What's happening? Why are your feet in the bathtub?" "Huh... we have.... Huh a little problem." Nurse Weezy shuts the door quickly. "Anne you tell me what's going on right now." Kate and Anne exchange looks, and both start babbling. "Stop! One at a time. Anne, you go first." "Ok, well do you remember Miranda?" "Yes, yes, go on." "She hates me and is collaborating with the evil Witch to destroy me. The Witch gave her a potion which she poured over my feet and now nothing will stay on them." Nurse Weezy puts her hand on her forehead "Oh Lord, and where is Cicero?" Kate explains, "Cicero has already gone to try and do something about this dreadful situation but he also has to help his friend, the man mouse." A puzzled Nurse Weezy cries, "What???" Xavier pipes up, "He went to save George." "Who is

George, Xavier?" "The man mouse. His name is George and the Witch turned him into a mouse. We help take care of him because he had no idea how a mouse lived or behaved and so we have been teaching him." A confused Nurse Weezy cries out, "You have been teaching a man how to be a mouse?" Xavier nods. "Lord have mercy! Ok I think we need to tell the King immediately." Kate, Anne and Xavier blurt out at the same time "NOOO!" In exasperation Nurse Weezy blurts out, "Please, don't you understand we need real help, we're not capable of dealing with this dilemma on our own." "Weezy, my Father will be so angry with me. We can figure this out just give us a few days. I am begging you to listen to us." "Oh child, why do I feel I'm going to regret this?" "Thank you, thank you Weezy, you won't regret it. I promise I won't let you down …. just keep everyone away while we deal with this." "On one condition Anne, you keep me up to date on everything and if I'm needed you come to me right away. Is that crystal clear." Anne agrees. "So be it!" declares Weezy. Princess Anne, Xavier and Kate all answer at the same time, "Clear!"

George and Cicero are both sitting in the cage with the cat staring at them. "I can't believe our bad luck Cicero. What on earth are we going to do?

Somehow, we have got to get out of this." "George, I told you not to worry, we're going to figure it out. That's right .... figure hmmm .... yeah, figure it out .... figure it out ...." At that moment we hear someone whisper, "Pssst, pssst! Cicero and George look down and to their great surprise see Xavier giving the cat a treat. The cat plays with it and paws it a bit, licks it and then devours it. Lazily the cat stretches and begins to get very sleepy. He tries to walk but stumbles wearily, sees double and then finally passes out. Xavier acknowledging his friends with a hopeful smile, quickly jumps on to the table pulls out a wire from his bag and begins picking the lock.

Miraculously, the cage door opens and Xavier urges, "Come on, come on, we have no time to waste!" and off they go squeezing through the tiny mouse hole and flying out the door. Five minutes later the Witch returns and finds the rascals have escaped. The enraged Witch tries desperately to shake the cat awake but alas, to no avail. He is out cold! The Witch wails, "Klinkety Klinkety Kats, all you rats!" At that moment all the rats appear from out of nowhere, she shrieks, "Don't just sit there you idiots, they have escaped. Now, go after them, move …. NOW!" The rats run out into the woods and are hot on their trail. Cicero yells, "My gosh, they are coming after us Ruuunnnn!" They run for their lives and thankfully find a small hole to dive into. Entering the opening, they soon find themselves tumbling and falling helplessly down, down and down into a deep dark hole finally landing in some kind of burrow. A ground hog pops up out of nowhere and scares them half to death. Feeling unsure and insecure about this strange fellow they wait for him to speak. He introduces himself to the group, "Nigel here." "I'm Cicero and this Is George and Xavier." Nigel sighed, "Got yourselves in a bit of a pickle, have you? Let me help you. Hop on." They all hop on his back and Nigel runs like the wind. The rats are scurrying frantically above the ground in a state of confusion. To their utter dismay, they have lost the scent and have no clue where to search. Meanwhile, Nigel stops for a moment to talk to the boys and explains, "I have a friend who can probably help you." Xavier asks, "Don't tell me! His name wouldn't happen to be Lachlann?" "You know him? Xavier replies "Know him? This is how it all got started. No thanks." Cicero jumps in, "Wait a minute now, I don't think we have a choice now, do we?" George agrees, "He's right, we don't have much of a choice and I don't want to be the pickle that's been eaten!" Nigel gestures for them to hop on his back again. He takes off like the wind running through a maze of tunnels like a roller coaster ride.

When he finally slows down and comes to a small doorway, they enter into the Wizard Lachlann's dorm where he is working on some kind of gadget. His hair is a mess and he looks like a crazy, mad scientist. He seems preoccupied but looks up and comments, "I see you brought some friends Nigel." "Yes, this is …." Lachlann stops him in midsentence, "Yes, I know them." Nigel, "That's funny, they said the same thing." "I don't suppose they blame me for all this mess, do they?" Without missing a beat, Xavier cockily pipes up, "You're kidding right, do you realize what you did?" Lachlann looks at him with a new respect, "I always knew you were a dark horse." "This has nothing to do with a horse!" He retorts impatiently, "Calm down Xavier! Do you want my help or not?" "Well, if it were ...." Cicero cuts him off and pleads, "Yes ... yes please, we would love your help." George chimes in "He's right, we need you." "Alright then, bring me up to speed." Lachlann sits and listens attentively while they go through the whole story. He ponders on it for a moment and then addresses them in a serious manner, "Ok, there's only one way to break the spells and get rid of that nasty Witch." They all perked up and listened very intently, "What's that?" "Hold on Cicero, I don't know yet!" "Lachlann, when will you know?" "Cicero, I have a few calculations to make and I will have the answer by tomorrow at midnight. Nigel will bring you to your rooms where you can eat and rest while I work this out. Believe me you'll need your rest." Nigel leads them to their quarters.

The princess is sleeping in the bathroom uhum, you know why and the sun is starting to come up. Princess Anne is sitting in a chair asleep with her feet soaking in the bath water. Nurse Weezy makes her way to the bathroom and sees Anne asleep. "Anne my sweet girl, are you ok?" Anne wakes up, yawns and stretches a bit. "Yes, I'm ok, I guess. Oh Weezy, what am I going to do? I can't live in a bathtub for the rest of my life." "Anne, where is Xavier?" Anne looks for him and notices that he's gone. Alarmed, she cries out, "Oh no, not him too! He did say that he had something to do. This is so awful I feel so helpless." At that moment she realizes that her stinky feet are far less important than the lives of her friends. "No! I'm not helpless, if I have to have these stinky feet then so be it. My friends and family mean more to me than some stupid smelling feet! I have an idea." Nurse Weezy shakes her head, "Oh no!" Kate comes up behind nurse Weezy and says, "Hello Anne how are you holding up?" Anne just gives her another one of her are you kidding me looks? Kate winces, "That bad huh?" "Yes, Xavier has gone as well." "Oh dear my poor friend." "I have an Idea Kate." "Oh no, really?" "Yes, I do Kate, we're going to face Miranda and find out what she knows." "I don't think so Anne! Who knows what she will do next" "Kate, she has already done what she's going to do, believe me she's scared to death by now because people like Miranda are cowards, and all cowards will cower under pressure." Nurse Weezy pleads, "Now wait just one second here, child I'm going with you." "No Weezy, you have to act as though everything is normal and Kate and I just went shopping and had some lunch." Kate agrees, "Anne is right, it might look suspicious if you were to come with us and its true Miranda is a coward." Nurse Weezy breaks out the nose plugs and hands them to the girls.

Miranda is pacing around her bedroom floor, "How could Kate have spotted me?   Of all the people ughhhhhhhh!"   She keeps hearing the Witch's voice, "Tell no one!" At that moment, a barefoot Princess Anne with Kate enter the door with clothes pins on their noses. Miranda cowers up into the corner. "What are you doing here and who let you in?" Kate angrily, "We let ourselves in." "You need to leave now before I yell, and have you removed. Oh my gosh, that smell!" She pinches her nose.

Princess Anne, "Try living with it! You call anyone, and I will tell them exactly what you did to me. My father will have you locked up for good, do you hear me?" "You heard what she said, now answer her Miranda!" She whimpers, "What do you want from me?" "What did you pour on my feet?" "It was just a joke Anne." Kate in a chilly voice says, "No it wasn't Miranda." "Ok I'm sorry I wish I could take it back." "Don't you think it's a little late for that?" Princess Anne agrees, "Yes, it is a little late, now start talking!" Miranda knows she has been cornered and there is nowhere for her to go. "Well, I was just so sick of watching you have the best of everything while it was so much harder for me! You wouldn't understand and so I went to the Witch for help to expose your problem then no one would like you. Anyway, you already had this problem and it's not like I gave it to you. I just wanted people to know the truth.   She told me ....." At that moment Miranda's door and windows slammed shut and the Witch suddenly appears in the room and glares at Miranda, "Not another word! Do you understand me?" They all look at her in shock as the Witch begins to fill the room with a smoky mist and as the mist fades, they all vanish!

The Witch has captured the girls and has them all tied up in her house while Miranda begs, "Please! I can't stand the smell." "The smell is the least of your worries. I, on the other hand, rather like it." Kate retorts, "You would." The Witch screams, "Quiet! You're right, I would since I created it in the first place." "The Princess stares at her in disbelief, "You're the reason I have stinky feet?" "Mmm, that will give you something to ponder upon." The Witch slams the door and locks it. The girls are frightened and are just sitting and staring at each other. Kate accuses Miranda, "I hope you know this is all your fault." "No, it's her fault. Obviously, her feet stink so badly because this Witch has a problem with her. I just happened to get caught in the middle of it."

"You're so selfish, we're in the middle of this and you can't find it in yourself to say sorry to Anne." The Princess grins from ear to ear as Miranda and Kate just stare at her in bewilderment. "She made my feet stink! This is fantastic." Miranda and Kate both blurt out "WHY?" "No! I don't mean that this is fantastic. Don't you see, the smell is not my fault. The Witch did it and so that means it can somehow be undone." Uncertainty and doubt cloud their faces.

Lachlann's Workshop...

Lachlann is working on some potion using some mad scientist looking machines. He stares into a chalice and finally looks up and smiles. Nigel calls out, "You have it? Have you?" "I believe I'm onto it! If my calculations are correct, and I do believe they are, then we will have it by midnight. The problem is we must get to the Three Stones in the woods and that's the tricky part." "Well, I'm sure you will have a plan by then. I'll leave you to it" and Nigel leaves.

Nurse Weezy is pacing the floor fretting about where the Princess is, "Why did I ever agree to this? Oh my, I should have made her tell the King. This is all my fault." Nurse Weezy heads to a closet in the hall and grabbing her coat she heads out of the house. She walks quickly to

Miranda's house where she is greeted by the maid, "Can I help you?" "Hi, I'm nurse Weezy, Princess Anne's nurse maid. I was looking for her and Kate. Are they here by any chance?" "Come in please! I will have a look." The maid leaves for a moment and then returns, "No, I'm sorry, it seems no one is here. Perhaps they all went out for a bit." Nurse Weezy thanks her and goes on her way. Now she is even more terrified and begins to run towards the woods where she finally finds the Witch's house. She snoops around the back and peers in a couple of windows until she comes upon the one where she sees the girls. Kate happens to be looking up when Weezy gestures her to be quiet. She pushes the window up and climbs in. Princess Anne is so surprised "Oh my Weezy, how did you find us?" "With fear and trepidation," she starts to untie all the girls and helps them climb out the window. They run as fast as they can through the woods when suddenly a black figure appears right in front of them and for a second, they fearfully think it's the Witch. Lachlann removes his hood and reassures the girls that he is a friend, "Follow me, it's your only chance." Trustingly, they follow him to his workshop. They are all standing there when Lachlann peers down at Anne's feet, "Oh dear, they really do smell quite dreadful." Nurse Weezy asks Lachlann, "Who are you and why are you helping us?" He goes over to a drawer and puts a close pin on his nose and Miranda begs, "Please, do you have another?" He throws them all one. "That's better. Now then Nigel, go and fetch the others!" Nurse Weezy asks, "Others?" They all have a puzzled look on their faces until Cicero, Xavier, and George are all brought into the room. The Princess cries out, "Cicero! I can't believe it, what are you doing here?" "I guess I have the same question." "You must be the mouse man I mean oh I'm sorry we have both been done wrong by that Witch." "Yes, we have." George turns to Lachlann, "Does it look like we have a plan?" As Lachlann hands the mice small clothes pins for their noses, he turns to the Princess, "No offense my dear girl, try not to take it personally. To answer your questions, yes, I'm just about finished so why don't you all go in the other room and when I finish Nigel will come for you. Go on now, I have lots to do." They all rise and go to the other room while Lachlann resumes perfecting the formula.

The Witch has now discovered they have escaped when she returns to the room where she imprisoned the girls and throwing open the door she stares crazily her eyes turning blood red with rage. The room is empty and upon discovering that her prisoners have escaped, she throws her head back screaming and laughing maniacally which could be heard echoing all throughout the land....

Queen Andrea is extremely worried. King Malcolm is reading a book in his study when she appears, "It's rather quiet tonight." "Yes Andrea, you're right." "Why is that?" "I'm not sure but it seems our little girl has been having quite the social life lately." "It's good to see her enjoying herself Andrea." "Yes, but I do worry about her just a little." "Well now my dear, it wouldn't be normal if you didn't but I'm sure she's having an adventurous fun filled time. She'll be fine." She stares out the window with a concerned look on her face. King

Malcolm tries to comfort her, "Now now dear she's a teenager and it all comes with the territory." "Yes Malcolm, I understand quite well but things have been much harder for our little girl." "Yes, you're right but now everything will work out just fine …. it always does." "But Malcolm that's what I mean, it hasn't been easy for Anne as she has had such a difficult road. Sometimes I wonder if this had anything to do with …" She composes herself as Malcolm looks at her quizzically, "What are you saying darling?" "Nothing, nothing at all, I'm just rather tired and need my rest. I am going to retire." "Alright dear I'm going to finish here, and I will see you shortly." He ponders over Andrea's words and begins to remember the Witch and how the knights burned her place down to the ground and sent her into exile. He keeps seeing her face and hearing her words over and over again, "Your children will suffer the sins of their Father." As Andrea sits in her room getting ready for bed, she remembers an argument with her sister over young King Malcom. "Seraphina why are you doing this?" "Doing what and why are you so consumed with what he thinks, you used to care about what I thought but now, it's only him that you listen to... I'm your sister and that should matter more." Andrea replied, "You are just jealous, I know it, I see it in your face, you don't care about me you only care about winning. "Oh wow! Why, you ungrateful little witch." "No Seraphina, you're the witch! Andrea walks out leaving Seraphina standing alone. Seraphina sneers, "I will show you a witch alright!" Andrea shakes her head from the memory and climbs into bed.

Back at Lachlann's Workshop. Everyone in the room is waiting with anticipation for Nigel and precisely at midnight, he walks in. "Alright then, everyone in the workshop." They all enter the workshop where Lachlann is waiting to talk with them. Nigel advises everyone to be seated while Lachlann walks up to Anne and puts something on her feet. He then removes his clothes pin from his nose and breathes. "That's better! As long as you wear this frequency oil it will contain the smell." A delighted Princess smiles as everyone removes their clothes pins. Miranda sighs, "Ohh, what a relief, thank goodness!" Lachlann shoots her a dark look as if to say be quiet. "Ok, I have good news and not so good news. Which one do you want first?" Nurse Weezy says, "The not so good." Cicero agrees, "Ok, shall we vote or does everyone agree?" Xavier impatiently goes off, "YES! YES! YES! we all agree, just tell us please." Lachlann walks over to a big pot where smoke is rising and a hologram image appears.

"You see these three stones, this is where it will all happen but first, in order for this to work we have to entice the Witch to the Stones which are located in the middle of the woods. However, there is a catch. The second part is it has to take place when there is a full moon which will not happen for five days. Anne exclaims, "Five days! We might not have five days!" "We have no choice and we have to use someone as bait. I know it sounds dangerous but once we have the Witch where we want her then we throw the potion on her and turn on the machine. The rest is history, she will be sent to another universe and the best part of all, according to my calculations every spell will be broken." George and the Princess both blurt out at the same time. "I'll do it!" "Well, you can both help, but I need to figure out a plan of how to entice her to The Stones. I have been working rather hard and I need to have some much-needed rest now." "Can we go home, or do you think it's too dangerous?" asks Anne. "No, my dear, you cannot! We can take no chances. We do not need any extra drama to interfere with our plans." Nurse Weezy is anxious, "He's right but we do have a problem because the King will send his men very soon to look for us if we don't return home." Lachlann puts her mind at ease, "After I have had a few hours of rest I will pay King Malcolm a visit at the Palace and fill him in on what has been going on and how we are going to make things right." Everyone looks rather dejected and concerned.

Lachlann goes to visit the King. Lachlann suddenly appears before the King while he is reading his newspaper. A little startled, King Malcolm remarks, "I see you're still up to your same old tricks. You know, you have a lot of nerve showing up here uninvited." "M'Lord, I can assure you that you will want to hear what I have to say in private." Lachlann stares at the butler and Malcolm nods to Potter to take his leave. "This had better be good Lachlann." The wizard takes his seat in the opposite chair and explains, "It's not about good or bad, it's about life or death and it involves your daughter." The king removes his glasses, puts his paper down and says, "You have my full attention." "Let me make this short and clear your daughter's condition came from a spell from the Witch. It seems she was rather upset about her new living arrangements. "What?" "Let me continue, Your Highness, there's more." "Please, tell me everything." "Your daughter has a friend who was quite jealous of her and went to the Witch to help her expose the Princess's unfortunate condition. In doing so, she caused a disastrous chain of events which resulted in Anne and her friends being compromised in an ugly way at the hands of this unhappy Witch who we both know. Your daughter, being your daughter, tried to clear things up with her friends but it all has fallen apart and they, together with Nurse Weezy are now in hiding at my headquarters." "Nurse Weezy? She's involved? I suppose you want something from me in return for your help?" "No, Your Majesty, I would just like to continue my work with your blessing and in answer to your question about Nurse Weezy, you are most fortunate to have such a loyal member of staff for it was she who saved your daughter's life." "Thank you Lachlann and I give you my word, if you can find a way to make this all go away and save my daughter and her friends, then you will have more than my blessing." "Your blessing is all I'm looking for." "Agreed." "Very well, I will keep you informed but it is best that you don't know the location for now." "Ok I'm trusting you." Lachlann stands and Malcolm shakes his hand warmly as he bows and turns to go while King Malcom stares at Lachlann watching him leave.

Everyone is waiting anxiously for Lachlann to return to the dorm and as soon as he arrives, Nurse Weezy asks, "Did you see the King?" "I did, and he's agreed to let me help. I will have a plan soon and we must all pull together as one team if we want to be successful. However, there is one exception, Miranda you have already proven yourself unworthy of such a task and you will remain behind because I cannot take a risk of betrayal of any kind from anyone." Miranda bows her head in shame and he adds, "Just so you know, if you are thinking of any funny business, let me remind you that the Witch will do away with you as soon as she can and believe me, she will! This is for the safety of everyone including you. Am I quite clear?" Miranda nods her head miserably. "When I have the plan together each of you will have a task to do and we will rehearse it numerous times until we know it like the back of our hands. We shall meet in the workshop at 8:00 tonight. I will see you all then." Lachlann leaves the room for a few hours and returns when rested. Everyone is in the workshop diligently doing their bit. Nurse Weezy is practicing with a rope, Princess Anne and George are pretending to talk in the center of the three prop stones, Cicero and Xavier are practicing the switches and levers, Kate is throwing something repeatedly while Nigel is carrying a rag in his mouth and helping Lachlann. Long periods of time pass and before they know it, two days have gone by. Lachlann finally calls for their attention, "You have all worked so hard and deserve a well needed break. Please enjoy dinner and take a nice long rest. Congratulations to everyone, you have all done very well." Cicero is holding court in the dining room with one of his stories which causes great laughter and fun while they all have eaten and enjoyed their time together. Lachlann raises his glass to make a toast, "Here! Here! to all of us, may we be blessed and have the light and luck on our side come the night of our dangerous ride." Everyone, "Here! Here!"

Back at the Palace, "Malcolm, have you seen Anne, I can't find her anywhere?" "Come in Andrea, my love, I need to speak with you."

"Malcolm, do tell me our daughter is alright?" "Yes my dear, our daughter is fine for now but she seems to have gotten herself into a bit of trouble. I am hoping it will all be sorted out soon." Fear creeps over Queen Andrea, "Where is she Malcolm?" Just then the doors fly open and in blows the Witch! "Yes, King Malcolm, do tell." Andrea gasps, "Seraphina? It is true you have completely taken to the other side. Why?" King Malcom angrily shouts, "How dare you burst into our private quarters, you wretched thing, you!" "The only wretched thing in here is you," sneers the Witch. King Malcolm calls, "Guards!" "They're all sleeping right now, they can't hear you. It seems there all out cold." She cackles cruelly. Malcolm moves Queen Andrea behind him and confronts the Witch. "What is it that you want Witch?" "Your daughter!" "Never! You old crone!" She whispers eerily, "In time .... In time." With a wave of her gnarled hand, she vanishes into thin air. King Malcolm sees Queen Andrea begin to sway and before she collapses, he catches her just before she hits the ground. He holds his wife gently while lovingly stroking her head and they find themselves completely alone.

Back at Lachlann's...

There is so much going on at Lachlann's house and everyone is hustling and bustling, talking nervously to each other, worried about what is going to happen next. Princess Anne feels so sad for George, "I can't believe that this happened to you. It must have been so lonely for you all these years." "Not any lonelier than it has been for you." "Why were you hiding from me George?" 'It wasn't you it was everyone because I was so embarrassed about my condition." "I know what that is like. What about your family?" "I left because I couldn't take the pain of seeing my parents suffer. I felt it was best for me to leave and so I ran away." "Why? Why did the Witch do this to you?" "Well, you see the Witch tried to trick me one day while

I was riding my horse down by the seashore. An old woman approached me asking for my help with her chores which I was very pleased to do. I was happily helping the old lady for many days until I found out who she really was. Alas, by then, it was too late and one day she captured me and tied me up in her house. After sometime she got fed up with me and turned me into a mouse. I returned to my Palace so that I could see my parents but when I looked down at my hands that were now paws, I realized I could not share this burden with them." The Princess is intrigued with George's story and asks, "How did you meet Cicero?" "Well, he would visit relatives from time to time and over the years we became friends …. just like you and Cicero." "I have never met anyone that knew just how I felt." "Neither have I Anne. Hopefully if all goes well, we will have our lives back, and the miserable old Witch will be long gone." "Oh, I do hope so George." "By now everyone in the room is tired and they all fell asleep.

It's now morning in the palace and the King and Queen are in their bedroom and Andrea is wondering what they should be doing to help. "Oh Malcolm, I feel as if we ought to be doing something." "We are my dear, we are! By staying calm and letting Lachlann quietly put his plan into action without anyone knowing, the less we do the less the Witch will learn. Do you understand what I'm saying?" "I do, but I can't help feeling like this is all my fault I want to do something. I hate this feeling of helplessness." Malcolm hugs his wife "I know my dear and it is certainly not your fault she chose her wicked path. Having patience sometimes is harder than any labor. It tests us in our most trying times. We are going to have to trust and believe that it is all going to work out. It has to, and it will." They hold each other and wait patiently for any news.

Meanwhile back at Miranda's house her mom Eleanor is in her room. She is looking for her daughter when one of the maids walks in. She asks her, "Have you seen Miranda?" "No Ma'am, I haven't but I believe she is with Kate and Princess Anne." Eleanor is pleased, "Oh good! Well, I'm off, I have a ladies meeting in half an hour."

Back at Lachlann's place everyone is busily packing and loading a large cart. Lachlann tells them, "We have approximately 48 hours until we must be in our places and please remember that this is our only chance. I don't want to scare you, but I must emphasize that we cannot afford to make a mistake here." They all agree and Nurse Weezy nods anxiously, "We understand, and we are quite prepared to give it all we have" "Thank you for all that you have done, and I know you will give it everything you have. We have all worked very hard to get where we are and I have complete faith in what we are about to do and what has to be done." Cicero is so relieved and tells Lachlann, "I cannot thank you and Nigel enough for all your help and risking your very own lives to help us." The Princess joins in "Yes, me too, I want to thank all of you for all your kindness and generosity and no matter what happens, I have never felt so blessed to be in such great company. I am so deeply honored by all of you and my heart has never been so full." George adds, "Since we're all getting so ... well .... I umm, feel the same way. I could not have a better or more loyal group of friends as I do at this very moment."

Lachlann stops them, "Alright, alright, back to work my friends, we still have a lot to do before midnight tomorrow. Everyone returns to work and gets busy for the upcoming adventure. Lachlann checks everything and tells them he will be back in a while. He goes to The Stones and takes a measurement then walks over to a tree, taps a sensor on it and as he leaves, he turns to survey the area. The sky is ink black and an eerie silence hangs over the Three Stones in the woods. With a shiver, Lachlann takes a last look and returns to the workshop, "We need one more person." Miranda feeling very ashamed of herself and her actions pleads, "Please …. Please …. let me, I beg of you. I know what I did was wrong, and I feel …. well I feel awful and if I could take it all back I would." "Yes Miranda, what you did was unforgiveable and totally disloyal however, I do need to be able to trust you one hundred percent and I am not at all convinced that I can do that with you." Princess Anne is listening to Lachlann's speech and feeling sorry for Miranda, she has a change of heart. "Wait, I believe her. Maybe she can help." "I can … I can … I promise you I won't do anything against you. I see now what true friendship is and what it means, and I want that too. I'm so truly embarrassed and ashamed of my behavior. I feel like this is my chance to make it up to all of you." The Princess agrees, "I believe her, and we do need another person." Lachlann reluctantly allows Miranda to help, "Very well, if we are going to allow her to do this, we have to get her prepared. Let me make this clear young lady, I will be watching you and if I see for one second that you're not honest, I will take care of you. Do you understand?" "Yes, I do!" She goes on to address everyone, "Thank you, I promise you all, I won't let you down." They recheck every detail of their duties for the difficult task ahead while

Lachlann works with Miranda showing her what she must do. It's evening and everyone is nervously gathered around the rather large fireplace except for Cicero who is pacing back and forth. Nigel begs, "Cicero, calm down old chap, what's gotten into that head of yours?" "It's just …. I have come up against her so many times and have always been defeated so I just want everything to go as planned. So yes, as you can see, I'm a bit on edge." A wise Nigel answers, "Listen, if it's worth anything to you we do have the master at hand. That's got to be worth something to you." "It is, it is." "Come on now Cicero, it's just a little stage fright." Princess Anne agrees, "I feel the same way. The thought of not having this problem is so exciting but I get scared that it might not work out and then where will I be? I guess the best way to deal with this is to only see and expect that it will be done." Lachlann walks over to them and says "Good advice Anne, that is exactly what one must do. Hang on to that and it will most likely see you through for only the masters have conquered such thoughtful meditation my dear." The Princess stares at him with complete understanding.

As we see the Witch making the Dreaded Potion she is pacing angrily back and forth muttering incoherently to her cat and her crow, "Hah! I'm going to catch that little girl and turn her into hmmmm! Now what would be fitting?" The crow screeches, and the Witch whispers, "You think so? Well that just might work." She dances and laughs giddily around her big black cauldron while stirring in her potions. The Witch chants, "Hubble bubble our Princess is in trouble and as it begins to boil a blue green mist rises out of the pot. In the mist a hologram appears of the Princess's feet and horror upon horror, they begin to turn into fins. Scales begin to form on her legs and her hips stopping at her waist. Oh, my Scotland! The Witch is turning the Princess into a mermaid! She pours the potion in a vial and running outside she grabs her crow with the cat following hot on their heels. Throwing the crow in the air she orders him, "Now go and find her." She then bends down to the cat, "You know what to do, don't mess it up, go on now!" The cat grabs the vial and runs off. The Witch laughs eerily echoing throughout the woods. George and the Princess are in the workshop thoroughly enjoying each other's company. She stops and asks everyone to step outside for some fresh air. They all agreed it was a good idea, but Lachlann warned them, "That's fine, but not too long and do not wander away from the building as we don't want anything to go wrong now that we are so close."

They all step outside for a moment to enjoy the sunshine. Everything seems fine but suddenly the crow appears in the tree and is watching them closely. The cat is approaching very quickly and runs up to the Princess, jumps up into her arms, drops the vial on the ground near her feet and a mist starts to rise. The cat jumps down and runs like a hare. The Princess falls to the ground and cries out, "Something is happening, help me!" Her feet turn into fins just as we saw in the hologram at the Witch's house. The Princess looks weak and George, along with the others are in shock. Lachlann comes running out and picks up the Princess carrying her back into the workshop and yelling to nurse

Weezy, "Start filling up the tub."
Nurse Weezy looks at the Princess
and wringing her hands she yells out,
"You have got to be joking …. Oh my
gosh! Oh my!" Lachlann commands
Weezy, "Pull yourself together now!"
He runs down the hall, enters the
bathroom and places Anne in the tub.
"Somebody get me some salt." Kate
runs into the kitchen and finds the
salt, quickly returning to the
bathroom and handing it to Lachlann.
As he pours the salt into the tub, the
life slowly seeps back into the
Princess. She weeps, "Oh my
goodness, I thought my stinky feet
were bad, but this is so much worse!
Oh dear, what shall I do?" As she
continues to cry Cicero, George, and

Xavier are sitting helplessly on the side of the tub just watching her. Cicero tries to comfort her, "Don't worry, it's just a storm in a teacup. We're going to fix this." She sobs harder and wails, "Everything is ruined and now I have destroyed our plan too." Lachlann silences her, "Listen Anne, I just need to make a few adjustments and I do believe she might have done us a favor." They all look at him in dismay, "HOW?" "I will explain soon but time is running out and if this is going to work, I must hurry. There is a large plastic tub in the other room, fill it with the salt and water and put Anne in it. We must get her to the ocean as fast as possible." Everyone is running around getting her ready. They lift her out of the bathtub, place her in the plastic tub and carry her onto the cart.

The Princess is now going into the ocean and darkness has fallen. They are all on the ocean shore and everyone carefully helps to put the Princess in the water. She yells with joy, "That feels so much better." She swims around for a little longer and resurfaces. Nurse Weezy asks her, "I hope you are not enjoying this too much now, are you? Your father and mother will have a fit and I will have to leave the country!" Princess Anne laughs as she says, "Oh I do like it you should try it sometime. This is like nothing I have ever known and in fact, I feel rather free." Weezy has a horrified look on her face. "Oh, don't worry Weezy, I would much rather be me but if I can't be me, this is really nice." Weezy looks relieved and Lachlann calls everyone over to advise them of the new plan. "I have to move the equipment over here and it will take about an hour or so. Everything stays the same except for you Anne. You will have to beach yourself a bit and cry, so the Witch can see you are in agony. Believe me, she wants to see this and that is why she will be here. The trickiest part of luring her to the Three Stones is over. She wants to see this, in all her madness. I will be back. Weezy, Miranda, come with me. The rest of you will stay here with Anne." As

Weezy and Miranda head back to the workshop with Lachlann, they stop on their way to the Three Stones to gather their gear. They then continue to the workshop to pick up all they need to fight the Witch. They load the cart and Weezy asks Lachlann, "Do you really think this is a better plan?" "Yes, I do Weezy. I can use the energy of the water to conduct the exact frequency I need." They head back to the beach where they set up the sensors and hide the machine. Lachlann walks over to the others, "Where is she?" George replies, "Well she keeps going out to sea. I believe she is exploring because she has been swimming the whole time." At that moment the Princess resurfaces and calls to Lachlann, "You're back? Is everything ok?" "Yes, but I need you to do something for me. You must stay away from the shore until you see me flash this light." He holds up a light and shows her. "Got it." "Ok my dear, go and enjoy yourself but don't go too far." She smiles and swims off under the water which she finds quite beautiful and marvels at all the living creatures around her. As she plays with the dolphins she encounters all different kinds of colorful fish including sea turtles.

The Moon is high and full, midnight is close, and the time finally draws near. Lachlann signals for her to return to shore. She pops her head out of the water, swims to shore and beaches herself on the sand. She bows her head and pretends to cry. The Witch appears and the sky starts to storm making the Princess a little afraid. "So child, how is the life of a mermaid treating you? Quite nice huh!" Anne trembles, "I'm not sure." "Well, your little Auntie has something even more fantastic to show you hahahahahaha." At that moment the water becomes rough and a very large ugly looking fin surfaces revealing a hungry great white shark! Sneering with a malicious grin as the Witch gloats, "It seems this boy's favorite meal is a mermaid. I have fed him quite a few." Princess Anne feels trapped and terrified. The Witch continues to cackle. Lachlann runs very stealthily to the other side of the beach where he signals to Nigel to hit a sensor and for Kate to run with the potion. George and Xavier are at the switches, Cicero is at the other sensor and Kate is close to the Witch. The Witch turns "Are you here to help your friend? Come along child, you are just in time for the show." Although Kate is trembling with fear, she is close enough to the Witch to throw the potion upon her. The Witch cries out, "What's this?" At that moment Nigel hits the sensor three times while George and Xavier pull the switches. Cicero hits his sensor, Lachlann and Miranda jump out with the machine and aims it at the Witch. A look of complete surprise, horror and fear come over the Witch's face as she fades like a smokey mist into oblivion. As the shark is about to lunge for the Princess, Weezy pulls her to safety. Magically the scales start to disappear, and Anne's feet return to normal. George miraculously returns to his handsome human self and runs towards the Princess crying "Are you alright?" "Yes, I am, oh my gosh, look at you! Is it really over?" Lachlann sighs with relief, "Yes m'lady, it is finally over." A roar of relief, pure joy and excitement floods the air. Miranda quips, "Is this really happening and is she really getting her handsome Prince now too?" Everyone at the same time "Miranda!" She bows her head,

"Kidding." They all head back to the palace and enter the doors bruised battered and wet having gone to war for the fight of their lives they all hug each other and are so excited for the success of their defeat against the Witch.

The good news has traveled throughout the Kingdom and everyone is in celebrations all around the Palace. Cities, towns and even the small villages enjoyed the festivities. At the Palace, King Malcolm addresses his guests, "Ladies and gentlemen, it is my greatest pleasure to gather you here today to honor my friend Lachlann for his loyal services to my family." As Lachlann stands before the King, he bows his head to receive the Medal of Honor around his neck and then Malcolm takes the ceremonial sword and taps each shoulder once. Arise Sir Lachlann! When the cheering and clapping died down, the King ordered everyone to eat, drink and be merry. George has been waiting in the background and nervously approaches the King, "I have something I would like to ask of you Your Royal Highness." "By all means my boy, please do." "I love your daughter and wish to ask you for her hand in marriage?" "You have my blessing young man, but I am sure my daughter is quite capable of answering for herself. I do thank you however, for honoring us and I wish you good luck." George bows and walks over to the Princess. The crowd senses something special is about to happen and becomes silent. Prince George kneels down on one knee and asks her, "My dearest Princess Anne, would you do the honor of marrying me?" "My dearest sweet George, of course I will." Everyone cheers and claps their hands as the King raises his glass for a toast, "To all my daughter's friends for being so loyal in helping to save her life and to Sir Lachlann for orchestrating such a complicated mission." Finally, he turns to his family and gives them a toast, "To my sweet wife, Queen Andrea, my precious daughter Princess Anne and

my future son in-law, Prince George."
The crowd cries "Hear! Hear!"

The wedding day has arrived, and people are celebrating throughout the Kingdom. The Palace gardens are overflowing with beautiful flowers and the tables are all draped in silver and white. Excitement ripples through the gardens as the guests await the arrival of the bride. Prince George is already standing with his groomsmen Xavier and Cicero looking very debonair in top hat and tails and the bridesmaids Kate and Miranda looking very pretty are also awaiting her presence at the rose bower. As Kate turns, she sees Prince Albert seated in the front row who grins and winks at her. A gentle blush comes over her face as she returns his smile. A hush comes over the crowd, the bugles sound and everyone gasps as they watch the beautiful Princess walk down the aisle with King Malcolm. The Stinky Feet are no more, and this gorgeous vision gracefully joins George in holy matrimony. Sir Lachlann is given the honor of performing the ceremonial vows, "Dearly beloved we are gathered here today in honor of Princess Anne and Prince George to join them in holy matrimony." He turns to George, "Do you Prince George take Princess Anne to be your wedded wife, do you promise to love, honor, cherish and protect her until death do you part?" "I do." He then turns to Princess Anne, "Do you Princess Anne take Prince George to be your wedded husband, do you promise to love, honor, cherish and respect him until death do you part?" "I do." Lachlann requests the rings and Cicero and Xavier each hand over a ring. Lachlann bends to receive the rings which they place in his hand and he winks at both of them as they bow and take their seats. "Take these rings and place them on each other's finger as a symbol of your love." George and Anne exchange rings and take each other's hands. "I now pronounce you man and wife. You may kiss your bride." They kiss then turn to their guests "Ladies and gentlemen I now present their Royal Highnesses, husband and wife, Prince George and Princess Anne." The crowd roars with excitement as they celebrate throughout the evening.

A year later Princess Anne and Prince George visit the Nursery where Nurse Weezy and Nurse Louise are leaning over the baby carriage. They are tending to the new little Prince with clothes pins on their noses. Fumes are coming off the beautiful baby boy's feet!!!!!   Cicero and Xavier exchanging knowing looks sigh, "Here we go again........."

The End

Written By

Jerri Renee

www.ingramcontent.com/pod-product-compliance
Lightning Source LLC
Chambersburg PA
CBHW070557180626
46817CB00005B/1884